A Place to Call Home

Alexis Deacon   *illustrated by* Viviane Schwarz

CANDLEWICK PRESS

What is this?

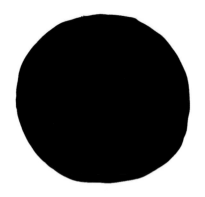

It is a small, dark hole.

It is also a home.
A nice, warm, safe home.

The
trouble
is, if you
grow up
in a small,
dark hole,

even
if
you
start
out
tiny,

there
comes a
time when
you've
grown
too big,

and
then
you
have
to
go . . .

out into the world.

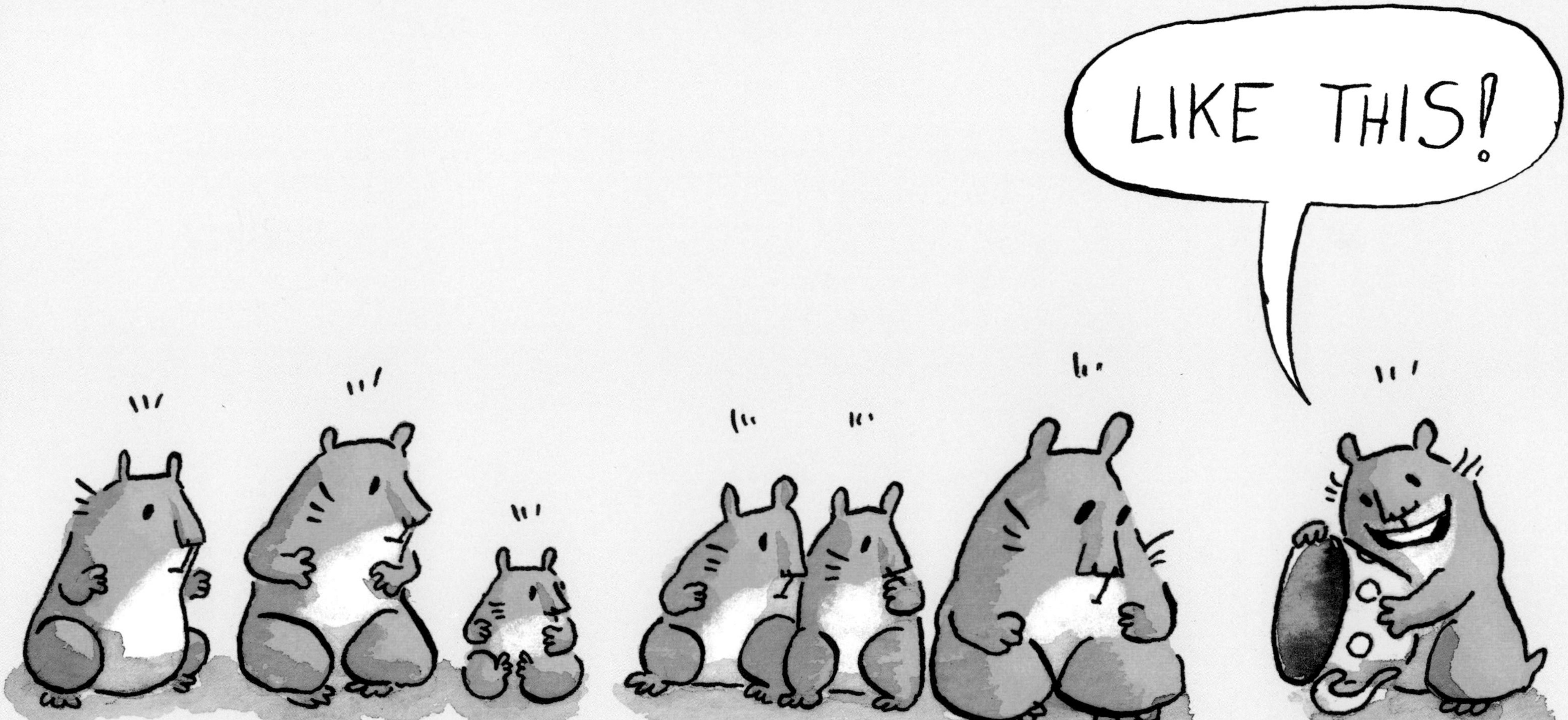
LIKE THIS!

And you can see where you're going.
So you can help us find a home.
OFF WE GO!

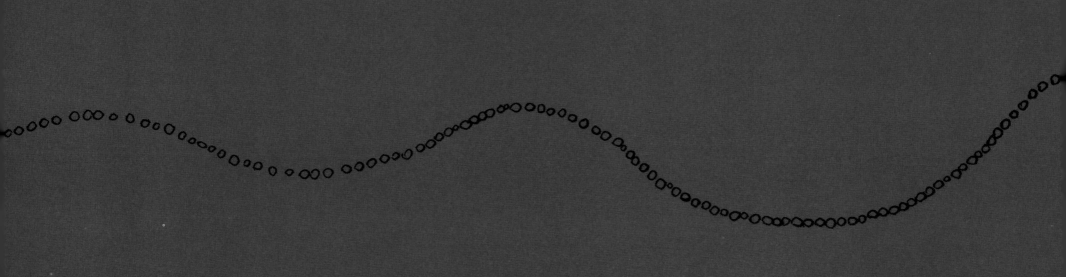

and it is home.

For Alice, my sister
A. D.
For my sisters, Ina and Silke
V. S.

Text copyright © 2011 by Alexis Deacon • Illustrations copyright © 2011 by Viviane Schwarz

First U.S. edition 2011

Library of Congress Cataloging-in-Publication Data is available.

Library of Congress Catalog Card Number 2010040125

ISBN 978-0-7636-5360-6

11 12 13 14 15 16 SWT 10 9 8 7 6 5 4 3 2 1

Printed in Dongguan, Guangdong, China

This book was typeset in Stempel Schneidler.

The illustrations were done in ink and watercolor and hand-lettered by the illustrator.

Candlewick Press, 99 Dover Street, Somerville, Massachusetts 02144

visit us at www.candlewick.com